The Adventures of
HENRY
WHISKERS

By **Gigi Priebe**   Illustrated by **Daniel Duncan**

WH15 K3RS

ALADDIN
New York   London   Toronto   Sydney   New Delhi

🪔 ALADDIN

An imprint of Simon & Schuster Children's Publishing Division
1230 Avenue of the Americas, New York, New York 10020
First Aladdin paperback edition January 2017
Text copyright © 2017 by Marjorie Priebe
Illustrations copyright © 2017 by Daniel Duncan
Also available in an Aladdin hardcover edition
All rights reserved, including the right of reproduction in whole or in part in any form.
ALADDIN and related logo are registered trademarks of Simon & Schuster, Inc.
For information about special discounts for bulk purchases, please contact Simon & Schuster Special Sales at 1-866-506-1949 or business@simonandschuster.com.
The Simon & Schuster Speakers Bureau can bring authors to your live event. For more information or to book an event, contact the Simon & Schuster Speakers Bureau at 1-866-248-3049 or visit our website at www.simonspeakers.com.
Book designed by Laura Lyn DiSiena
The illustrations for this book were rendered digitally.
The text of this book was set in Vendome ICG.
Manufactured in the United States of America 0317 OFF
10 9 8 7 6 5 4 3 2
Library of Congress Control Number 2016932136
ISBN 978-1-4814-6575-5 (hc)
ISBN 978-1-4814-6574-8 (pbk)
ISBN 978-1-4814-6576-2 (eBook)

For David, Haley, Chelsea, and Hunter.

How did I get so Lucky?

I Love you more than you wiLL ever know.

CONTENTS

✤ PREFACE ✤

IN A DIMLY LIT ROOM, INSIDE A CASTLE, perched high on a hill above the River Thames in England, sits a dollhouse. This dollhouse isn't for dolls. It isn't even for children to play with. It has four floors, forty rooms, two working elevators, hot and cold running water, and electricity. There's a grand marble staircase, a kitchen with shiny copper pots, a garage filled with luxury cars, and toilets that really flush. There are even crystal chandeliers that twinkle, a grandfather clock that chimes, and a phonograph that plays records.

This dollhouse is like no other—and it was never meant to be. It was made for the queen of England, who loved collecting miniature objects and tiny things. Hundreds of the country's finest craftspeople were called upon to create

1

dollhouse-size copies of everything found in the grandest homes of England. Nothing was overlooked; no detail was too small. Even the books in the library were written by England's best-known writers and poets.

The dollhouse is more than eight feet long, four feet wide, and five feet tall—and it was made to travel. When it was finished and moved from place to place, its precious furnishings were safely stowed in little cedar drawers built into its base. Its first trip was to London, and then it was taken throughout the English countryside and put on display. When its traveling days were over, it came to rest in the dimly lit room at Windsor Castle, where it lives today.

The castle has sky-high towers and turrets and is surrounded by a moat. The dim room, on the first floor of the castle, has decorative molding and dark wood floors. In its center, the dollhouse sits on its base, elevated to eye level so visitors can easily look inside.

Nearly a million people come to see the dollhouse year in and year out. But what they can't see are the drawers in the base hidden from view. Emptied of their contents and tucked safely out of sight, they make the perfect place for a family of mice to call home.

✦1✦
NARROW ESCAPE

IN THE BLUISH-GRAY LIGHT OF EARLY
dawn, a young mouse slept soundly, cupped in the
cushion of an old leather armchair. His long, sleek
tail dangled limply over one side while a front
paw draped across his charcoal brow. On the floor
at the foot of the chair lay a book with its pages
opened to a picture of a medieval knight dressed
in a suit of armor.

Henry Whiskers felt as if he were a thousand

miles away, floating in a dream. It was a happy dream, and he began to chuckle—until something interrupted it.

"*Psst!* Henry! Henry! Wake up!"

Henry didn't budge.

"Henry! You have to get out of here!"

Henry slowly opened one sleepy brown eye, then the other. He smiled and yawned. He uncurled himself and stretched, shaking out his paws. Just before he closed his eyes once more, he noticed the form of a familiar mouse in the distance. Jeremy.

"Henry!" pleaded the squeaky voice. "It's getting light out, and Warden will see you! Run!"

This time, Henry's heavy eyelids snapped open and he bolted upright. Warden was a tour guide. Panic gushed through him, and he scrambled off the chair and scurried across the floor.

"The book, Henry! Pick up the book!" Jeremy waved his big paw frantically through the air.

At that very moment, Henry saw a light flick on in the surrounding exhibit room. He almost somersaulted over himself as he skidded to an abrupt stop and turned around. His heart sank to his feet. He'd forgotten to put the book back on the bookshelf. And now Warden was at the entrance to the exhibit room.

Henry dove onto the floor and slid over to the book on his soft, white stomach. At that same moment, Jeremy retreated up the dollhouse chimney and out of sight.

In one swift move, Henry lassoed the book with his tail and raced up the shelves. He jammed the book back into the empty-toothed gap it had left and raced back down.

Crouched under a footstool, Henry waited for Warden to put out the wooden sign letting visitors know that the famous dollhouse exhibit was open. When his cue came, Henry made a run for it. And as he ran, he promised himself over and over that he'd never sneak into the library again as long as he lived.

Henry could hardly breathe by the time he met up with Jeremy near the fireplace.

"Did he see you? What happened out there?" whispered Jeremy.

"No. I mean, I don't know," gasped Henry, panting hard.

"What do you mean you don't know? How can you not know?"

"I don't know. It was all a blur."

A long silence followed as they thought about the possibilities.

"We better get home," Jeremy said, "or someone will definitely notice we're missing."

Henry cast a quick glance back over his shoulder. The hair at the back of his neck bristled, and he clamped a paw to his mouth.

Jeremy followed Henry's gaze. "Is that . . . ?" squeaked Jeremy.

Henry nodded, and then, as if Jeremy was reading his mind, the two of them high-tailed it out of the library, down a long hallway to a back set of stairs. Just before they plunged down the steps, they held each other back with a forepaw. A four-legged shadow with an upright tail slowly crept across the floor just below them. They spun around and darted through the pantry, leaped out of the house, and streaked across the exhibit room floor. They dove through a heating grate on the far wall and dashed down toward the ancient tunnels that weaved through their world beneath Windsor Castle.

✦2✦
WHO CAME FIRST?

JEREMY WAS ONE OF HENRY'S COUSINS, and there were a lot of those in the Whiskers family—149, to be exact! Keeping track of who was related to whom was confusing. All Henry knew was that he and Jeremy were best friends and both related to Great-Great-Grandfather Whiskers, who'd lived a long, long time ago.

"How did you know where to find me?" asked

Henry, zigging and zagging through a tunnel with Jeremy.

"Where else do you go at night?" squeaked Jeremy, leading the way.

It was true, Henry thought, remembering the first time his father had taken him to the library to read him a bedtime story.

The Whiskers lived aboveground in the storage drawers of the dollhouse. Other families of mice nested in the underground, below Windsor Castle, where they spent their days sniffing and scavenging for food, stuffing and fluffing their nests, and meeting up at the King's Crumb or, if they were young, the Neighborhood Nibble. Luckily, cracks in the floorboards were wide enough to slip through to reach the underground, which made it easy to see friends and relatives. But there was one serious rule of caution in Henry's family. Until the castle was closed at the end of the day and no visitors or wardens were around to discover them, Mother Mouse insisted that Henry and his siblings stay out of the dollhouse—including the library!

"Good point," said Henry as he and Jeremy followed the out-of-the-way trail back to Jeremy's.

"Besides, you were supposed to spend the night at my house, remember?"

"Oh, yeah. I guess I fell asleep."

"Obviously!" Jeremy said, rolling his eyes and smiling. "It's not exactly the first time," he panted. "You better watch out, Henry, or one of these days, you're going to get caught."

Henry paused to think about what would have happened if Jeremy hadn't come looking for him. He shuddered. Mother Mouse always warned them: "If they find one of us, they will look for all of us." The thought of being "the one" to cause a mouse hunt was too much. Henry forced himself to think about something else.

"Hey, Jeremy, do you know the story about the very first Whiskers to live in Queen Mary's Dollhouse?"

"I kinda forget," said Jeremy. He could add and subtract faster than just about anyone, but remembering things like history wasn't one of his stronger skills. "Tell me again."

As the two mice scurried toward Jeremy's house, keeping a careful eye out for any early-morning rat risers, Henry began to tell Jeremy the story of their famous ancestor.

"You know why he was called Henry Whiskers the First, don't you?"

"Because somebody had to be the first?" Jeremy replied hopefully.

"Sort of," said Henry. "It was actually because Henry was the first mouse to ever live in the dollhouse."

"I knew that," said Jeremy, perking up as he began to remember the story. "Wasn't he the queen's pet or something like that?"

"He was her son's, Prince George's. The prince loved him so much that when he grew up and moved away, he secretly placed Henry in the dollhouse to live for the rest of his life. The prince knew that Henry would be grateful and take good care of it. And every generation of Whiskers afterward became the caretakers of the house," Henry explained.

"Which are you?" asked Jeremy, pausing to pick up a crumb. "How many Henrys have there been?"

"I'm the twenty-fifth," said Henry.

"But how did the prince expect Henry the First to take care of that mouse mansion all by himself?"

"I guess Prince George thought that Henry the First would find a Mrs. Henry to help."

Henry and Jeremy stopped talking and slowed

down. They'd reached Rat Alley, the border between mice and rats. Henry never understood why, but he'd been told that "mice live in the castle's Upper Ward and rats live in the Lower Ward. That's just the way it is!"

They began to tiptoe and pay closer attention. They tried to quiet their breathing so they could hear if anyone might be lurking in wait for two unsuspecting mice. Henry cocked his ears back and forth as they crept along in suspicious silence.

This new tunnel gave Henry the shivers. It seemed particularly dark, and the stench in the air told him that they were well beyond their normal boundaries. "I don't like this," Henry whispered. "We should turn around."

"Don't worry so much," said Jeremy, waving away the idea with his paw.

Henry kept following. He held a paw to his nose and tried to ignore the knot in his stomach.

15

"How can they stand the smell?" Jeremy said, half gagging.

Henry carefully picked his way through slimy food scraps and smelly garbage that littered Rat Alley. Trying to sidestep some of it, Henry lost his balance. All four paws flew up in the air, and he landed on his back with a *thwunk*.

"Did you hear something?" Jeremy whispered over his shoulder, not even noticing Henry.

"What gave you that idea?" muttered Henry, scrambling to his feet and scurrying to catch up with Jeremy. "I really think we should turn around."

"Why? We're almost . . ." But Jeremy's words were suddenly drowned out by a horrifying, high-pitched, ear-shattering screech that pierced the air behind them.

"Run!" squeaked Henry, turning to see two enormous ratty eyes racing toward them.

Without hesitation, Jeremy and Henry picked up their tails and darted through the tunnel. The snarling sound grew louder as the giant rat gained on them.

In their panic, Henry and Jeremy made a wrong turn. By the time they realized it, it was too late to go back. Stealing a quick glance over his shoulder, Henry saw that Jeremy was falling behind and that the rat was only ten mouse-lengths away.

"The pipe!" yelled Henry. "Run for the pipe!"

With only a few inches between them and the rat's razor-sharp teeth, Henry lunged into an old drainpipe and Jeremy scrabbled in right behind him. They slid to the bottom and flew out the end, landing back in mouse territory.

"Mouse munch!" hissed the rat after them.

With his heart pounding in his ears, Henry looked back up the black iron pipe and saw that the rat was stuck, too fat to fit through its opening.

"Whew! That was close!" Jeremy said, exhaling loudly and wiping his sweaty brow.

Just out of the corner of his eye, Henry thought he saw something move, but when he turned to look, there was nothing there. "Did you see anything?" he whispered, placing a trembling paw on Jeremy's shoulder and nudging him away from the spot. "Let's get out of here."

"We can't go home looking like this," said Jeremy, pointing a black sooty paw at the filth that now coated Henry's fur.

"We could go to the Local Drip and clean off," suggested Henry. "It's not too far from here and on the way to your house."

"Yeah. Let's go," squeaked Jeremy, taking the lead again.

Even though there was barely enough water to get clean, it was enough to wash off the worst of the grime.

"We just need to dry off a bit," said Henry.

"Run around in circles for a minute!" said Jeremy. So they made a game out of chasing each other's tails while they air-dried.

"Good enough!" hollered Henry just as Jeremy was about to grab his tail. The two inspected each other from head to paw and then took off for Jeremy's house.

THAT TIME OF YEAR

THE SMELL OF CRUMB CAKES CAUGHT Henry's attention as he sat in Jeremy's bedroom, gently rubbing the stiff spots on his body and inspecting his bruises.

"Your house always smells like something good to eat," he said, carefully stretching his hind legs.

Jeremy stuck his nose out from under his covers, where he'd been dozing, and sniffed the air. He sprang to his paws announcing, "We'd better get some before they're all gone."

Henry smiled to himself. Jeremy was never one to miss out on a chance to eat when nibbles were near. Scootching to the edge of his chair, he cautiously placed one paw on the ground and then another, slowly testing his sore limbs before following Jeremy into the kitchen.

"What's the matter with you?" squeaked Aunt Begonia, wiping her paws on her apron and tousling Henry's hair as he passed by.

Henry loved Aunt Begonia like a second mother. She always liked to spoil him with attention and extra helpings of everything. He could hardly remember a time when she wasn't wearing her polka-dot apron around her plump white belly, mixing munchies and sampling sweet temptations in her kitchen. Most went with Uncle Charlie to be sold at the King's Crumb, but she always kept some for family and friends.

"We need to put some meat on your bones," she squeaked as she waddled over to him and held a platter of fresh crumb cakes in front of her.

"Fine by me," he said with a smile, wondering if she'd noticed how late he and Jeremy had gotten home. He helped himself to a pawful of his favorite cakes oozing with blueberries and sat down quickly to sink his teeth in before she could ask any questions.

While Henry and Jeremy quietly gobbled down their breakfast, Uncle Charlie appeared after a long night's work at the King's Crumb. "Just saw your mum, Henry," he announced when he saw Henry sitting at the kitchen table. "She stopped in for some of my famous cheese balls."

"Whose?" Aunt Begonia teased.

"Yours, my love. And aren't they scrumptious." Uncle Charlie winked at Henry.

He tossed his tweed hat on the table and was just

about to pull up a stool beside Henry when Aunt Begonia stopped him short. "They make hooks for hats, dear, now please set a good example for our boys."

Uncle Charlie cupped a paw around his mouth and tilted over toward Henry and Jeremy. "She's got eyes in the back of her head, boys. Can't get away with anything anymore." He chuckled, went to hang up his hat, and then sat down next to Henry.

"Where was I?" He scratched his head. "Oh, yes. Your mum." Then he pounded a paw on the table and started to laugh out loud. "She had Tudor and Thomas with her doing some early morning errands. She sure does have her paws full with those two terrors, doesn't she?" he asked of no one in particular. "I don't know what they did this time, but that mother of yours grabbed each one by an ear and marched them out of the Crumb as quick as they came." Uncle Charlie paused. He began

twisting his whiskers thoughtfully, as though trying to figure out where Thomas and Tudor went
wrong.

"I wouldn't want to disappoint that one, if you
know what's good for ya," he said, chuckling again,
and slapped Henry on his aching back. He meant
Mother Mouse. She expected her children to behave,
be kind, be helpful, and stay out of trouble. "Which
reminds me to remind *you* for *her* that you've got
some chores to do at home, so you'd better not dilly-
dally around here too long." And with that, Uncle
Charlie's whole face seemed to disappear as he bit
into Aunt Begonia's blueberry crumb cakes.

Henry rolled his eyes. "It's that time of year
again," he mumbled through a mouthful of cake.

Uncle Charlie smiled knowingly, poured himself a hot cup of mint tea, then stirred it two times
to the right and once to the left before plucking
some crumbs from his whiskers.

"Time for what?" mumbled Jeremy through bulging cheeks.

"How could you forget?" squeaked Henry. "It's time for the queen's royal birthday banquet and the Whiskers' Annual Mouse Masquerade." It was the one time of year when it was safe for the Whiskers to throw a party in the dollhouse. While the queen and her guests partied upstairs in the castle's ballroom, the Whiskers could open their doors to friends down below.

"Oh, I knew that!" Jeremy piped up.

Henry heaved a heavy sigh as he bit off another piece of crumb cake. Entertaining in the dollhouse meant a lot of chores for Henry and his brothers and sisters, especially without Father. "Mother Mouse has us clean the dollhouse from top to bottom, not to mention raid the castle pantries twice as often."

"Sounds delicious," said Jeremy, licking some

stray crumbs from his whiskers. "It's not as if we get to raid the royal kitchens as often as you do. You practically live in them!"

"Yeah, but it's risky business. There are always more cooks in the kitchens during banquet season. And then there's Titus, prowling around like he owns the place."

"He's been a menace to mice as long as I've been alive," Uncle Charlie chimed in. "Never knew a nastier cat!"

Jeremy propped an elbow on the table and rested his chin on his paw, gazing upward dreamily. "Wouldn't it be nice to have all those butlers, chambermaids, housemaids, cooks, and chefs taking care of your every need?"

"Yeah. I wish they'd clean *my* house!" grumbled Henry, washing down the last of his crumb cake with a drop of thistle juice.

"Think you'll be conducting a pantry raid

today?" Jeremy asked hopefully. "Can I come?"

Henry shook his head. "How can you still be hungry?"

Jeremy just shrugged his shoulders and smiled. "It comes naturally."

"I don't know what Mother Mouse has in mind, but whatever it is, it would be a lot more fun if you were with me."

So Henry and Jeremy left for the Whiskers', but not before Henry remembered to thank Aunt Begonia and get one of her special nuzzles.

It didn't take Henry and Jeremy long to get there. The old tunnels below Windsor Castle crisscrossed deep underground from one end of the property to the other. The tunnel that Henry and Jeremy were following ran right below the dollhouse. As soon as they reached the right spot, they crept up a well-worn path through the floorboards and into the Whiskers' cedarwood home. They'd hardly emerged when they heard the sound of thundering paws and squeals of laughter.

"Quick, Henry, save me!" squeaked Isabel, Henry's littlest sister, who was playing "cat and mouse" with James and Albert, the identical twins.

If there was a runt in the family, Isabel was it. Everything about her was tiny, from the tips of her little ears down to her dainty paws. Even her whiskers were more delicate than most. But for every inch of her, there was tremendous speed, and that made her especially good at the game she loved so much. Most of the time, she was able to escape capture by hiding in small places where her brothers couldn't fit. If worse came to worst, she'd act completely helpless and close to tears so Henry would feel compelled to save her.

As Isabel grabbed Henry around his middle, she

spun herself behind him, putting him between her and her pursuers.

"No fair," squeaked her brothers. "You're trapped. We got you. You're it!"

"Am not!"

"Are too," echoed the "cats."

Henry called for a time-out and said they couldn't play if everyone was going to argue about the rules.

"Isabel," he said, "sometimes the mouse gets caught. There are no safeties in this game. It's all right." Henry leaned over Isabel to reassure her. He noticed her whiskers begin to quiver. "It's only a game." He picked her up, stroked her silky coat, and whispered three little words in her soft, pink ear: "Never give up!"

As soon as he placed her on the ground, and before the others knew what was happening, Isabel dashed off.

"You haven't got me yet!" was all they heard fading into the distance as they hightailed it after her.

Henry and Jeremy scampered down a long, narrow hallway toward Henry's bedroom. Everyone had their own storage drawer for a room, so no two looked alike. Mother Mouse encouraged each of her children to decorate their room any way they wanted. She called it "self-expression." Of course, they had to come up with the decorations themselves, but that was half the fun.

As they passed by Henry's oldest sister's room, Jeremy stopped to stare. His eyes grew wide as he wondered aloud, "Doesn't Regina ever get sick of pink?"

"You'd think," Henry snickered.

"Where does she find it all?" asked Jeremy.

"Mostly from the queen's wardrobes." Henry gazed at the sea of pink feathers, pink toenail polish, pink rose petals, pink hand soaps, and a pink ribbon taken from one of the queen's hats. And then there was Regina's favorite: a pink powder puff, which she slept on.

"The queen must like pink a lot too," muttered Jeremy, shaking his head.

"Regina says it's mostly 'raspberry,' and she does." Henry nodded. "Now you know why it's Regina's favorite color too. If it's good enough for Her Royal Highness, then it's good enough for Her Royal Headache."

Henry and Jeremy chuckled as they rounded a corner and entered Henry's room. It had a bed made from cotton balls, cattail fluff, and shredded tissue paper. There wasn't a single patch of wall that wasn't covered with wrappers, tour guides, shopping lists, ticket stubs, and gift shop receipts. But in the very center, right above his bed, was a clipping from the local newspaper, the *Royal Rag*. It told of a tragic event that happened when Henry was Isabel's age. It served as a constant reminder of his father and everything Henry hoped to be when he grew up.

Devastating fire swept through the castle and took the life of one of our own . . . , the article read. *But thanks to the heroic efforts of Mr. Henry Whiskers, the lives of a Mrs. Myrtle Mouse and her children were saved. Tragically, Mr. Whiskers, well known for his generosity, died while leading others to safety. Mr. Whiskers was the twenty-fourth heir to Queen Mary's Dollhouse and the first to hold the Annual Mouse Masquerade for the entire community. He will be sorely missed by one and all.*

The article went on to list the names of his father's loved ones, but young Henry could never quite get through this part. The words always got too blurry. His heart felt as if it would burst every time he read it. Not just because it pained him so much, but because it made him so proud. It inspired him to be the best mouse he could be.

<h1>→ 4 →</h1>

<h1>WARNING SIGN</h1>

WHEN HENRY AND JEREMY REPORTED TO Mother Mouse in the kitchen, she was giving directions to Isabel. "If nobody's home," she said, reaching for a sack with her long, elegant paws, "then leave the invitation at their door and move on." Mother Mouse gracefully crossed the floor and placed the sack of invitations at Isabel's feet.

"I know what a big girl you are, but I'm sending Albert and James along so they can help carry the bag." Mother sneaked a wink at the boys.

This was the first time young Isabel was allowed to go out to do errands on her own. She beamed proudly as Mother Mouse kissed her on the cheek and sent the three of them on their way.

Mother Mouse went over to the kitchen table and checked something off her list, then turned to face Henry and Jeremy.

"Jeremy's offered to help with my chores," Henry told her. "What would you like us to do?"

"Your choice," said Mother Mouse, smoothing her black-as-night fur and looking down at her list again. "Only a few days left until the party. The cars still need to be polished, floors need to be swept, and pillows need to be plumped."

Henry and Jeremy exchanged smiles. "We'll take the cars," they said, and went to gather some rags.

They set off for the dollhouse garage, where

a collection of six cars was parked, each looking exactly like its life-size version in the queen's royal fleet.

It was late afternoon, and Windsor Castle was now closed to visitors. Henry knew that Warden usually went home after closing, so nobody was likely to be lurking about in the dollhouse room. But that didn't guarantee that it was safe.

"Any sign of Titus?" asked Henry, knowing how the savage tabby cat liked to stalk the castle.

"He's probably busy coughing up a fur ball," Jeremy scoffed.

Easy to joke, thought Henry, *when we've never actually run into him.* And he hoped they never would!

When the two mice were certain that the coast was clear, they entered the dollhouse garage. Along with the cars, there was a bicycle, a motorcycle, and a gas pump.

"Where should we start?" asked Jeremy, clapping his front paws together. But before Henry could answer, Jeremy leaped up and into the red leather driver's seat of a black convertible. He threw his rag down and gripped the steering wheel with both paws. Henry watched as Jeremy made rumbling sounds, pretending to drive.

"Don't get any ideas," hollered Henry, poking his nose over the hood of the car. He knew that look on Jeremy's face all too well. Sometimes he got carried away. "We've got work to do."

"Aw, come on, Henry. Tell me you don't think it would be fun to take it for a spin," Jeremy dared Henry. "How many mice have a garage full of cars that actually work?"

"No, Jeremy!" said Henry.

"Why do you always have to be so responsible?" grumbled Jeremy, climbing out of the car and slamming the door behind him. He stomped away from Henry to the opposite side of the car.

Henry stopped polishing and looked over at his best friend. "Hey, in case you've forgotten, I nearly got caught last night, remember?"

"Yeah, well, I know you're the oldest in your family and everything, but you have to have some fun *sometimes*!" Jeremy kicked a tire.

He has a point, Henry thought.

Silence hung in the air as Henry pushed his rag all around the hood of the car in rapid, repetitive circles.

"You have to admit, Henry, it would be *really* fun," Jeremy yelled over the car.

As Henry worked his rag down the smooth, sleek side of the car, he tried to picture himself behind the wheel, whizzing through Windsor Castle's corridors. That was definitely not on Mother Mouse's okay list!

"Maybe," he mumbled faintly.

"You mean it?" Jeremy shouted. "Would you ever really give it a try?"

"Maybe," Henry repeated.

Jeremy snorted slightly and shook his head at Henry as if he didn't believe him. Henry didn't know whether to be hurt or offended. He decided to ignore Jeremy and blew a little puff on the rear fender creating a foggy patch, then rubbed it out. And that's how the two of them continued until they had finished with all of the cars.

Henry straightened a side mirror with his tail. "I guess that about does it," he said, standing up on his hind legs to inspect their work. The light danced off of every bumper, headlight, hood, and rooftop.

"We make a pretty good team," squeaked Jeremy, rubbing his stomach.

Jeremy's words made Henry feel better somehow. Maybe Jeremy wasn't too disappointed in him after all.

"I'm hungry," Jeremy said with a yawn.

"No kidding," Henry teased.

"What time is it, anyway? Seems like we've been here forever."

"I think we have," said Henry, feeling a little hungry himself.

"Want to go to the Neighborhood Nibble?" asked Jeremy. "I bet everyone will be there."

"You're probably right," said Henry, picturing everyone packed under the roof of the rusty old strainer that had been saved from the royal rubbish years ago. Its glimmering lights and nibbles-to-go made it so popular—and loud! Not peaceful like the library.

Between the two of them, Henry was usually the party pooper, but he didn't want to give Jeremy another reason to pick on him. "I might come in a bit, but first I think I should go to the library and double-check to be sure that I didn't leave the book sticking out or something. You go ahead, and thanks for helping."

Jeremy's mouth curled as he turned and waved good-bye with his rag.

"It's not what you think," Henry yelled after him, but he knew his friend had sniffed right through his excuse.

"Don't fall asleep this time," Jeremy hollered over his shoulder before disappearing from sight.

Henry scampered up the marble staircase of the dollhouse. The stone felt cool and soothing to his sore paws. When he reached the second floor, he skittered into the library and took a long, luxurious sniff. He loved the rich smell of its wood-paneled walls and leather-bound books that lined the walnut shelves. On the floor, next to the chair where Henry liked to read, stood a big spinning ball that showed a map of the world. Henry had never been outside Windsor Castle, but his father had once told him that the world was very big and full of mysteries. Henry didn't know what mysteries were, but he wanted to try some.

In the middle of the room stood a mahogany desk that Henry especially loved. Its drawers were filled with stationery, and on top lay some beautiful pens. It looked like it was just waiting to be put to good use.

He thought for a moment about sitting there but couldn't resist a good read. He climbed up a few shelves and lassoed his favorite book with his tail, then slowly lowered himself and the book to the floor. Once he'd scampered up into the armchair, he reeled the book up after him. With book in paw, Henry flopped onto his back and slumped into the hollow of the cushion. He spread himself across the chair, resting his head on one arm and his hind paws on the other. And then he began to read. He read for hours. He hardly moved except to tickle his ear with the tip of his tail.

Henry was just about to close the book for the night when he suddenly heard two voices.

"You're working awfully late," boomed one of them.

Henry's heart jumped into his throat. *Not again,* he thought.

"Just roping off the doorway to the exhibit before the morning rush," replied the second voice.

Henry recognized one of the voices as Warden's, whose job it was to tell visitors about the dollhouse and answer their questions. But why was he here when the castle was closed? Henry sat up, peeked out from behind the tall back of the chair, and cocked his ears.

"You're going to disappoint a lot of tourists, mate," said the guard as he read a new sign that Warden placed at the entrance to the exhibit room.

"I'm afraid so," agreed Warden, "but it's got to be done."

Henry's ears perked up. *What's got to be done?* The second that the guard and Warden left, Henry hopped out of the chair and grabbed the book. He wasn't going to forget it this time! He practically threw it back on the shelf, then raced to the safety of the fireplace to make his way down the chimney to the ground floor. Taking his chances, he darted out onto the wide-open floor of the exhibit room and raced over to the sign that Warden had put out. When he reached it, he stopped. Instinctively, he sniffed left and right to make sure that no one was coming. Then he turned to look at the sign, twirling his tail nervously around a paw as he read:

DOLLHOUSE CLOSED FOR REPAIR
OPENING AGAIN SOON

How soon? Henry wondered. He didn't understand. "Why would they do that? There's nothing wrong with it," he said to no one. *This is bad,* Henry thought. *What if someone saw me last night after all?* He started to panic. *What am I going to tell Mother? What about the Mouse Masquerade?*

Henry picked up his tail and darted back home. It was late, and everyone was sound asleep when he arrived. He'd lost track of time. *No point in telling them now,* Henry decided, so he dragged himself to bed wondering what Mother Mouse would say when she heard the news in the morning.

⤙5⤚
TOO LATE

"WHAT'S TAKING SO LONG?" HENRY hollered, tapping a hind paw impatiently. He could never understand why girls took *forever* to brush their teeth and comb their coats in the morning. He was just about to pound on the door for the third time when it flung open and Victoria and Caroline giggled right past him, as if he were invisible.

"Finally!" he muttered sleepily as he side-stepped his sisters' things scattered on the floor.

He'd barely gotten the toothpaste on the brush when the door behind him flew open again.

"Henry, Henry," shrilled Regina. "Henry! Come quick!"

Henry rolled his eyes and started brushing his teeth.

"Henry! This is serious! Isabel's missing!" she shouted, yanking on his arm.

He stopped to spit and turned to look at Regina. Her whiskers were quivering.

"What do you mean she's missing? Where is she?"

"If I knew that, she wouldn't be missing," hissed Regina hysterically.

Henry blinked the sleep out of his eyes. Before he knew it, all of his brothers and sisters were crammed in the doorway. Albert and Caroline rubbed their paws nervously while the others clutched their tails and looked to Henry for answers. He gulped hard.

"We were playing cat and mouse while Mother was out," sobbed Beatrice.

"What time is it? Where were you playing?" he asked.

"What difference does that make? Isabel's gone!" Regina shouted, flapping her paws every which way.

"I got that!" Henry snapped. "Just tell me what time it is and where you were playing."

"It's ten a.m., and we were playing in the dollhouse!" Beatrice blurted.

Henry raced out the door while the words trailed after him.

This is my fault, thought Henry. Then, just as he was about to climb up the chimney into the dollhouse, he heard voices from above. Next came scraping sounds, thumping and bumping. He turned on his paws, ran back, and slipped through the hole to the underground. He made his way under the floorboards and popped up behind a heating grate on the wall of the dollhouse room to see what was going on.

He peered out from behind the grate and swallowed hard as he watched a large man pluck items from the dollhouse with white-gloved hands. Henry scoured the growing collection of furnishings that were being placed in a bin: dressing tables, wooden bed frames, washstands, a trouser press, a chest of drawers . . .

"That's a very good question," Henry heard Warden say. Henry leaned out of the grate just enough to see Warden standing at the exhibit entrance on the far side of the room. Warden was bending over a sad-looking child, explaining, "No, we don't have to close the house very often, but it's the queen's birthday in a few days, and we want to make some repairs and polish it up so the whole thing looks like new."

"Look at this," Henry heard the repairman say to Warden.

"What do you have there, Freddy?" Warden straightened up, patted the child on the head, then walked over to inspect the crystal mirror that Freddy held in the palm of his hand.

"What does that look like to you?" asked Freddy, pointing to something on the mirror.

Warden put his glasses on to examine the mirror more closely. "Well, I'll be," he said. "It looks like a tiny paw print!"

Henry felt sick. He tried to control the nervous tapping of his paws. He wished Jeremy were there.

"Imagine what a wonderful story that would make," Warden continued.

"What do you mean?" Freddy scratched his head.

"Imagine if the dollhouse was full of mice," Warden said. "Can't you see it now? A family of mice living like royalty, bathing in marble bathtubs, dining off fine china, and sipping wine from the cellars?"

Henry's legs buckled beneath him.

"That *would* make a lovely little tale!" Freddy replied. "Get it?" He doubled over laughing. "A lovely *tale*, like T-A-I-L!" the guard said. Warden chuckled, then quickly collected himself and went to greet another tourist.

Henry watched anxiously for hours as the repairman removed item after item from the dollhouse and Warden comforted disappointed visitors. Finally, Freddy stood up and invited Warden to join him for a short tea break.

This is my chance, Henry thought as the two men walked out of the exhibit room. He sprang out of the heating vent and streaked across the floor. In an instant, he was inside the dollhouse, desperately squeaking Isabel's name as he ran.

Henry decided to work his way from the top of the house to the bottom. He searched the foyer before running up the grand marble staircase. When he reached the top floor, he darted into the nursery, where his siblings loved to play. Everything was gone! The toy train, the piano, the merry-go-round—even the tins of tea and biscuits! It was clear that Isabel wasn't there.

Then Henry searched through the king's and queen's bedrooms, where nothing had been removed. He lifted each silky bed skirt and peered underneath. He opened closets and drawers, searched behind cupboards and chests, but Isabel was nowhere to be found.

Time was running out. Henry could feel it as

his chest heaved with every frightened breath. "Isabel!" he called, darting in and out of the bathrooms. "Isabel! Are you in here?" When there were no more rooms to check, Henry stopped dead in his tracks. A terrible thought occurred to him. He peered out of the dollhouse to search for signs of Isabel in the half-filled bins left on the exhibit room floor far below.

Just then, the doors to the exhibit room opened and Warden was back. Henry slipped out of sight, down through a crack in the floorboards of the dollhouse and back to his lookout behind the heating grate in the wall.

"But we've come so far," Henry heard someone say when he reached the heating vent. He turned and saw that Warden was speaking to an elderly couple.

"I'm terribly sorry," said Warden apologetically.

"When will it reopen?" asked the elderly man. He held a cane in one hand and his wife's arm in the other.

"I'm afraid not for a few days," said Warden, sounding rather sad himself.

"We won't be here that long," said the woman. "I've waited all my life to come to England and see Windsor Castle and this famous dollhouse."

"Excuse me, just a moment," said Warden, taking a step farther out into the corridor and looking left and right. "I think we can make this one exception," he whispered, removing the rope. "I really shouldn't be doing this, but it's almost closing time anyway, so I'll just shut these doors and no one will see us."

"Oh, you're a dear," trilled the woman as she and her husband shuffled into the room.

"You'll have to excuse our appearance," Warden

explained. "I'm afraid that some of the rooms have had furniture removed."

The couple didn't seem to care, Henry noticed, as they stared wide-eyed at the dollhouse.

"Is it true that everything really works?" asked the man, hunched over his cane.

"Yes, it is," said Warden with pride. "Even the wine in the wine cellar is real."

Henry watched impatiently as Warden walked the couple around the dollhouse. They peered into every nook and cranny, oohing and aahing. When they were stopped in front of the library, the woman frowned slightly and stared at something intensely.

"Look!" she said, pointing a shaky finger. "That little book is upside down."

Henry felt dizzy, then everything suddenly went black.

⇥ 6 ⇤
PRECIOUS CARGO

HENRY BLINKED AND RUBBED HIS EYES WITH his paw. He found himself slumped over with his face pressed against the heating grate, so he pushed himself back into a sitting position. Just as he realized that he must have fainted, he heard the repairman and Warden talking.

"Don't forget to leave that sign out again for tomorrow," said the repairman, pointing at the **CLOSED FOR REPAIR** sign. "We'll be at this until

Her Majesty's birthday," he told Warden, who nodded.

He watched intently as the repairman placed the grandfather clock in a bin along with some chests, trunks, and the library desk. Then it hit him. Henry knew where Isabel must have hidden during the game of cat and mouse! Afraid to move now, Henry remained frozen in his spot.

When the bin was full, Freddy announced, "This is the last of it for today. I'm just taking this to the workshop."

"I'm leaving too," said Warden. "It's time for me to go home."

Freddy and Warden marched off, bin and all, leaving the cars and other random items on the floor outside the dollhouse. Henry's whiskers quivered and tears welled in his eyes as he stood on his hind legs watching. Every hair on his body told him to follow the bin. *She's got to be in there,* Henry said to himself as he leaped out of the hole in the wall and onto the wide-open floor.

Henry hugged the walls, careful to keep out of sight. He hoped that he blended in well enough with the castle's dark brown floorboards as he dashed out of the exhibit room.

Freddy led him through the room next door. The floor was suddenly carpeted, and brightly lit cabinets towered above Henry on either side, displaying the queen's collection of fine china. There were no more shadows to hide in.

While he was trying to formulate a plan, it occurred to him that he could just be on a wild-goose chase and that Isabel might still be back in the dollhouse.

Suddenly, Henry didn't know what to do. But before he had time to decide, something colorful caught his attention at the far end of the hallway. It was Titus!

He had short orange fur, steely gray eyes, sharp-looking white teeth, and claws that clacked on the hard floor. He was nearly as big as the queen's dogs, but a whole lot meaner.

Luckily, he hadn't seen Henry—yet! And for the briefest moment, time seemed to stand still . . . until Titus stopped in his tracks, with one front paw suspended in the air. Then he lowered his tail, cocked his ears forward, and charged toward Henry.

This is it, thought Henry. He whipped around and ran the other way.

"Blimey!" Freddy hollered from behind.

There was a sudden chorus of hissing, snarling, and shouting followed by loud crashes and clangs. Henry dared to cast a quick glance over his shoulder. Warden had slipped into an elevator while Freddy had tripped over Titus and was now on his knees, bent over gathering bits and pieces of dollhouse furnishings scattered on the floor. Henry's heart nearly stopped. Desperately, he searched for signs of Isabel as Titus retreated.

When Freddy put the last item in the bin and walked down a staircase toward the basement, Henry didn't dare to follow.

A cat may have nine lives, but a mouse only has one, and I need help, Henry thought as he hightailed it to find Jeremy.

+7+

A FRIEND IN NEED

HENRY TRIED TO APPEAR CALM WHEN HE
ran into Uncle Charlie, who was heading to work
at the Crumb and tipping his hat politely at a lady
mouse passing by them.

"I think you'll find Jeremy at the Nibble," said
Uncle Charlie, reading Henry's mind.

"I should have known," mumbled Henry as he
waved good-bye halfheartedly and turned in the
other direction.

"But, Henry," Uncle Charlie called after him, "your mother's worried about . . ."

Henry didn't hear the rest. He ran like the wind to the Nibble.

"Where have you been? I've been looking for you all day," Jeremy asked, pointing his tail accusingly at Henry when he appeared at the hangout. "Her Royal Headache sputtered something about Isabel gone missing."

"No time to explain," Henry panted, beckoning Jeremy to follow with his paw. Without waiting for a response, he turned and took off.

"But where are we going?"

Henry was in too much of a hurry to answer. He could feel Jeremy close behind. Just knowing he was there made Henry feel better . . . braver . . . stronger. He ran on, leading Jeremy through familiar tunnels and finally up a heating duct that led back to the castle hallway.

"Why are we here?" asked Jeremy.

Henry put a paw to his mouth, signaling Jeremy to keep quiet. Peeking out from behind the heating grate in the wall, he sniffed for signs of Titus and any other threat that might be lurking about.

"He took her through here," Henry whispered. "I lost him, though."

"Who?" Jeremy asked. "Who took who?" He paused. "Isabel?"

Henry nodded before squeezing through the grate onto the carpeted floor.

Jeremy leaped out, landing beside Henry.

"Isabel?" Jeremy asked again.

"Yes!" shrieked Henry in a panic. "He took her! She's gone! I've lost her!"

Jeremy's eyes were wide and his mouth hung open, speechless.

"He went that way," Henry finally managed to say, pointing toward the far end of the room with the queen's china and the staircase beyond.

"Who's he? Who went that way?"

"The repairman named Freddy," Henry shouted, as if Jeremy should already know. "Follow me," he said, starting for the distant stairs.

But before the two mice reached the staircase, Freddy and a small army of men in green uniforms just like his walked in.

By now, Henry and Jeremy were in plain sight, right in the middle of the massive carpet. Instinctively, they crouched, frozen in place. If they made a dash for it, they would attract attention.

"Stay still," Henry whispered to Jeremy, wishing the men out of the room.

Henry and Jeremy had no choice but to watch and wait.

"I say we roll it from this end and work our way in that direction," said one of the men, waving his finger.

"I say we roll it from both ends and meet in the middle," said another.

Henry stole a quick glance at Jeremy, who looked equally confused. He could only hope that he and Jeremy were camouflaged against the patterns and colors of the rug. There was nowhere to hide.

"Climb the wall!" Jeremy squeaked frantically.

"They'd see us for sure!" Henry squeaked softly. "Let's lay flat, keep still, and hope they don't notice!"

Those were Henry's last words before the rug came rolling toward them from both sides and he and Jeremy were swallowed up.

Henry was sandwiched between layers of carpet. He could hardly breathe. This was a tight spot, even for a mouse. He tried to talk, but he was so flattened, he could barely open his mouth.

"Jeremy?" he managed to mumble. "Are you there?"

"I'm here," came the muffled sound of Jeremy's strained voice.

"I think we're moving," Henry tried to yell, but it came out as only a stifled squeak. He could hear the muted voices of the men around him and felt himself being jostled with the rug as he and Jeremy were carried off.

✤ 8 ✤

PICKING UP THE TRAIL

WITH A VIOLENT JOLT AND A LOUD *THUD*, they came to an abrupt stop. Henry felt sick. He needed air. He needed to get free and back to searching for Isabel!

He listened as well as he could, still trapped within the rolls of the rug. The sound of the men's voices seemed to be fading, as if they were walking away.

Henry tried to wriggle himself free. He heard

the faint sound of Jeremy doing the same.

Progress was slow, but eventually, Henry sniffed fresh air. It took every ounce of strength, but once he reached the outer edges of the rug, he was able to squirm out.

"Help me," squeaked Jeremy, poking his snout out.

Henry pulled Jeremy's paw hard. With one big yank, the two tumbled back onto a concrete floor.

"I feel like I've been flattened by a rolling pin," groaned Jeremy as he tried to get up.

"Come on," Henry coaxed. "We've got to get out of here. If we don't hurry up and find Isabel, it will be too late."

"We'll find her," reassured Jeremy.

Henry wanted to believe his friend, but it was hard.

Henry looked around the windowless room. It was filled with nothing but rugs rolled up into enormous sausage shapes and placed in perfect rows. He and Jeremy zigged and zagged up and down the rows until they found a doorway that led out to a brightly lit corridor.

"I think we're in the castle basement," Henry whispered.

Slinking along one wall, Henry and Jeremy cautiously made their way down the corridor. There was a long line of lights running down the middle of the ceiling above and several doorways on either side of them.

"She's got to be here, Jeremy," said Henry. "She's got to be in one of these rooms!" He was getting excited now. "You take that side," he said, pointing to the doors on the left, "and I'll look in these."

"What am I looking for?" asked Jeremy.

"Things from the dollhouse . . . or the big bins that they put things in."

"Got it," said Jeremy, dashing into the closest room.

Henry and Jeremy skittered in and out of the rooms, announcing what they'd found each time they completed a search.

"We're running out of rooms. We've got to be getting close," Henry hollered as he raced through the second-to-last door on his side.

In a flash, Henry dashed back into the hallway and yelled out to Jeremy. Jeremy poked his nose out of the room across the way.

"Quick!" Henry rapped his paw anxiously on the ground. "Over here."

Henry led Jeremy into the room that must have been the repair shop he had heard Freddy mention earlier. Empty bins were stacked on the floor, but what caught Henry's attention was the familiar chime of a grandfather clock that he recognized from the dollhouse. It could barely be seen, standing on top of a long worktable in the middle of the room. From down on the floor, Henry couldn't see anything else on the table, but the clock was enough to suggest that more things from the dollhouse might be up there too.

"Be careful," Jeremy warned as Henry placed his paws on the table's cold, steel leg. Henry was weak from wriggling out of the rug, but he managed to hoist himself up to the top without falling. The table was covered with dollhouse furniture, toys from the nursery, and tins from the food pantry—but there was no sign of the suitcases and trunks that Henry suspected Isabel might be hiding in. Droopy whiskered and disappointed, Henry turned to climb back down.

But then he heard it: a sniffle. Faint at first, it got louder as Henry tiptoed through the collec-

tion, twitching his ears back and forth to deter-
mine the direction of the sound.

"What do you see?" shouted Jeremy from
below.

Henry didn't answer. He was busy listening
for the sound again. It was coming from behind a
wardrobe. Henry ran around it and saw a tall stack
of brown leather suitcases.

"Isabel, are you there?" he cried.

Nothing.

"Isabel?" he called again, desperate to hear her
voice. More silence followed. He stood still and listened. He heard a slight *plink*. "Izzy, are you there?"

"Henry!" he finally heard his sister squeak. "Get
me out! Get me out!" Her voice was coming from
a tan leather trunk at the bottom of the stack of
suitcases. Henry dashed over to it and saw a gold
key lying in front of it. He sniffed around the
shiny keyhole.

"I'm here, Izzy. I'm here!" He was so relieved that he started to laugh and cry at the same time.

"Henry, I've been so scared," Isabel cried. "I thought the trunk was locked, so I pushed the key in, but it won't open."

"We'll get you out," Henry promised. "Jeremy is with me. Hang on. I'll be right back."

"Don't leave me!" Isabel blurted.

"I'm not leaving you. I'm just going to tell Jeremy I found you. Don't worry."

Henry skittered to the edge of the table and yelled down to Jeremy, who scampered up the table leg quick as a flash. When he got to the top, he fixed his eyes on the suitcases that towered above them. Henry could tell what Jeremy was thinking.

"Let's give it a try," said Henry. And with that, they placed their paws up against the bottom suitcase and pushed with all their might. It wouldn't budge.

"What's happening?" squeaked Isabel through the keyhole.

Henry let out his breath and wiped a paw across his brow. "It's not locked, but there are a lot of suitcases stacked on top of the trunk you're in. That's why you couldn't open it. We need to push them off." Henry tried not to sound worried. He poked Jeremy and threw his paws into the air, unsure what to do next.

"Am I trapped?" asked Isabel, starting to cry.

"You're not trapped," Henry said, sounding more confident than he felt.

"Look," shouted Jeremy, trying to drag something long and shiny over to the trunk. "Maybe this will help."

Henry saw that it was a human-size letter opener. It was tremendous and barely budging with all of Jeremy's effort!

"How's this supposed to help?" Henry asked.

"We'll stick it under this bottom suitcase and pry it up so all the other suitcases slide off. Then we can push the bottom one off and open the trunk."

With the two of them hauling the letter opener over to the stack of luggage, Henry and Jeremy were able to wedge its tip under the suitcase and push down hard on the other end. The stack didn't move.

"Let's lean into it with our shoulders," Henry suggested, but that didn't work either.

Jeremy nervously twisted his whiskers, and Henry wrung his paws.

"This isn't going to work," said Henry. "We need more power to push or pull this stupid stack over."

"I've got it!" Jeremy clapped his paws. "But you're not going to like it."

"Why not?" asked Henry. "How do you know?"

"Because it involves taking something that isn't ours," said Jeremy.

"But why?" Henry asked, sounding desperate.

"Because it's the only way," said Jeremy, very convincingly.

"Only way to what?" they heard Isabel whimper from the keyhole.

"To get you out of there," Jeremy answered.

Henry twirled his tail around and around while he looked back and forth between Isabel's large brown eye peeking out from the keyhole and Jeremy, standing with both paws on his hips waiting for Henry's decision. He surrendered.

"Okay. What do we have to do?"

✦ 9 ✦

MISSION IMPOSSIBLE

THE DOLLHOUSE SPARKLED LIKE A JEWEL lit from inside and twinkling in the middle of the darkened exhibit room. It was well past closing time at the castle and all the staff had long gone, so the coast was clear for Henry and Jeremy to sneak out. To Henry's relief, the cars were still there on the exhibit room floor, reflecting light off their polished hoods.

"Someone sure keeps this fleet looking shiny," Jeremy joked.

Henry snickered, then nervously focused on the cars.

"Which one do you think we should take?" he asked.

"The motorcycle with the sidecar would be fun," said Jeremy.

"But there wouldn't be enough room for all three of us," Henry pointed out.

"Oh, yeah. How 'bout the town car?" Jeremy suggested. "Then we could ride in style like the queen."

"Too big," Henry said, walking toward a sleek car called the Silver Ghost.

"Humph!" Jeremy snickered, crossing his front paws and shaking his smiling face at Henry. "This is a first!" he mumbled under his breath as Henry climbed into the driver's seat.

"What do you mean?" asked Henry, running a paw around the smooth steering wheel. "I know it's not ours, but we need it to save Isabel."

Jeremy nodded in agreement, then smiled and jumped into the front passenger seat as Henry searched for the starter button.

"Do you know what you're doing?" Jeremy asked as the car rumbled to a start. "Can I drive on the way back?"

Henry could tell Jeremy saw this whole thing as one grand adventure, but this was serious! They had to get to Isabel before someone else did! He slowly inched the car forward, then it gained speed as it rolled out into the middle of the room.

"Watch out!" shrieked Jeremy as Henry frantically spun the wheel left and right, just missing a wall. The little car whizzed and bounced over a nubbly red rug that led from one room into the next. Henry was getting the hang of it.

When they reached the staircase at the end of the corridor, Henry braked hard at the top.

"What do we do now?"

They both peered over the dashboard and down the long, steep staircase. There were no lights on at the bottom, so it looked like the stairs fell away into a bottomless hole.

"Hold on! This is the only way," said Henry as he pressed the accelerator to the floor, hurling the car over the edge. Bumping and bouncing, the little car shot down the stairs, soaring over several at a time while Henry and Jeremy hollered at the top of their lungs. With a hard *thump*, the car landed on the floor at the bottom. Henry braked and stopped the car long enough to find a knob that turned on the car's headlights. "Okay," he said to Jeremy, driving forward again, "now we can see where we're going."

"You sure you've never done this before?" yelled Jeremy, grinning from ear to ear.

Just as they were rolling past one of many offices off the hallway, Henry thought he heard something.

"Did you hear that?" he asked, turning to look at Jeremy. He slowed the car to listen.

"It sounds like someone's hurt," said Jeremy.

Thinking only of Isabel, Henry panicked and turned the steering wheel hard to drive in the direction of the sound. When they reached a doorway in the middle of the hall, they saw Titus, sitting with a tiny rat pinned beneath his paw. Henry hit the brakes, stopping before Titus noticed them in the doorway.

"This doesn't look good," whispered Jeremy.

Henry's mind was racing. His eyes darted around the room, and he lifted his nose, as if a clue might be found floating in the air. "That rat's just a baby!" he said.

"Come on, Henry! Get out of here before Titus comes after us!" Jeremy pleaded.

"We need to *do* something," said Henry. "We have to help him." Henry changed gears and slammed the pedal to the floor. The car shot forward.

"What are you doing?" screeched Jeremy, grabbing the dashboard and closing his eyes.

The car barreled into a wastebasket, but Henry didn't let up on the pedal. The engine strained while the tires spun, but the wastebasket slowly began to move. Henry kept at it, sliding the can along the floor until it finally tipped over.

Frightened, Titus jumped out of the way just long enough for the little rat to run for cover.

Henry put the car in reverse, then spun it around and raced out the door.

"Is he chasing us?" Henry hollered over the whisker-whipping wind in his face.

Jeremy checked the side-view mirror and looked out the back of the car.

"Not yet, but let's not make any more unnecessary stops."

Henry nodded as they zoomed along, heading for Isabel.

"Wait a minute," shouted Henry, suddenly remembering a long piece of carpet string he had seen earlier. "One last stop," he promised as he pulled up to the heap on the floor. "Open your door and grab that. I have an idea."

Jeremy leaned out his door, snatched the wad of string, and shut the door as fast as he could.

Henry put the car in high gear again, then hollered "Hold on!" as he made a sharp turn back into the repair room, where Isabel was waiting. Before he could put a paw on the brake, they crashed into a table leg. One of the headlights broke, and the engine sputtered to a stop.

"Wow!" exclaimed Jeremy, straightening his whiskers.

"Isabel, I'm here!" panted Henry, racing up the table leg. "Are you all right?" he puffed, skittering to the keyhole.

"I thought you were never going to come," Isabel squeaked, frightened, from inside the trunk. "Can you get me out?"

"We'll have you out in the twitch of a tail," said Henry. Then he scampered halfway down the table leg and hollered to Jeremy. "Hey, throw me the string."

Jeremy leaned into the backseat to pull it out. He tossed one end of it up to Henry, who lassoed it with his tail.

"Tie your end to the front bumper," Henry shouted as he clambered back up the leg.

Pulling himself up on top of the table, Henry turned and waved down at Jeremy. When Jeremy gave Henry the paws-up sign, Henry dashed over to the trunk and climbed up the stack. He carefully wrapped the string around the handle of the top suitcase, tied a knot, leaped down, and darted back over to the edge of the table to signal Jeremy.

"Now what?" Jeremy yelled between his paws.

"Start your engine!" hollered Henry.

"*Brilliant!*" Jeremy shouted back. He jumped into the driver's seat and put the car in reverse. The top suitcase flew off the stack, whizzing over Henry's head as it sailed off the table and crashed to the floor.

"It worked!" Henry hollered, clapping his paws. Then they repeated the whole thing again.

One by one, Jeremy and Henry moved the suitcases off the trunk. Finally, Henry heaved open the trunk's lid and held it just long enough for Isabel to scramble out.

"That sure was a good hiding spot," said Henry, wrapping his paws around his sister.

Isabel buried her face in Henry's shoulder and cried with relief.

"I did what you always tell me to do, Henry," she sniffled.

"What's that?" he asked, nuzzling her head.

She stepped back and wiped her wet cheeks. "I didn't give up," she said, beaming proudly.

Henry got a lump in his throat. "Good job," he said, pulling her back to him for another tight squeeze. "You're the bravest girl I know," he told her.

Together, they scurried over to the edge of the table. "I'll lead and you follow," said Henry as he started down the table leg.

When they reached the bottom, Jeremy clapped his paws and hugged Isabel. Her eyes lit up when she saw the car.

"Oh, Henry. It's beautiful!" she said.

"We've got to hurry, Isabel. Mother will be frantic about us. You hop in the back," said Henry. "It's safer back there, and I need Jeremy up front to help navigate."

Jeremy held the back door open for Isabel and bowed just like the queen's chauffeur. Henry scurried around the car to take the wheel while Jeremy jumped into the passenger side. The next moment, they were speeding down the hall headed for home, laughing and cheering the whole way.

✦ 10 ✦

ON THE WAY HOME

ISABEL SQUEALED WITH DELIGHT EVERY time the car hit a bump and she was bounced up and down in the backseat.

"Hey, my turn to drive," said Jeremy.

"Oh, yeah. Sorry 'bout that. Let's switch places," said Henry, slowing the car to a stop. He slid over to the passenger side as Jeremy hopped out to run around the back.

"Can I try too?" asked Isabel eagerly.

"I think you've had enough adventure for a while, Izzy," said Henry.

"Well, we're about to have another!" exclaimed Jeremy as Titus suddenly pounced into their path.

"Watch out!" screeched Isabel.

Jeremy ducked as Titus's razor-sharp claw lashed out, missing him by a whisker.

Henry shimmied back over to the driver's seat. "Jump into the back," he hollered at Jeremy.

Isabel shrieked as Jeremy threw himself in and Henry floored the gas pedal. Titus erupted with hisses and took off after them.

"We're going to run out of hallway," screamed Jeremy, waving a pointed paw over Henry's shoulder at the wall ahead. At that same moment, Henry saw the wall getting closer and closer. He yanked the wheel back and forth, trying to buy them some time, but it was no use.

"Brace yourselves!" yelled Henry, slamming on

the brakes, which threw the car into a stomach-sickening spin. He fought for control, frantically turning the steering wheel around and around.

"Straighten her out!" screamed Jeremy, clutching the back of Henry's seat. "Don't stop or we'll be mouse meat!"

The car felt like it was about to flip, but Henry held the wheel steady, managing to steer them out of Titus's reach. They sped down the darkened hallway and took a sudden turn into one of the rooms.

"Why'd you do that?" yelled Jeremy. "There's no way out!"

"Yes, there is," squeaked Isabel. "Look!" She pointed excitedly.

"Where?" Henry yelled back to her.

"Over there!" yelled Jeremy, pointing over Henry's shoulder. "Behind that pipe."

Henry turned the car slightly until the one

working headlight shone on a gaping hole in the wall behind a rusty radiator. "Think we can fit?" Henry hollered.

"It's going to be close!" shouted Jeremy.

"He's coming," squeaked Isabel, looking back at Titus.

Henry gripped the wheel firmly with one paw, covered his eyes with the other, and gunned the engine. When he opened his eyes, they were on the other side of the wall in pitch blackness except for the car's headlight. Seething hisses trailed after them, and when Henry turned around, he could barely make out the shadow of Titus's paw poking desperately in and out of the hole in the wall. That was the last thing he saw before the rats.

✦ 11 ✦
RAT ALLEY

"GO BACK! GO BACK!" JEREMY SHOUTED.

The car slid sideways before skidding to a stop right in front of a pack of rats. Everyone held their breath and stared ahead.

Ten bloodred eyes zeroed in on the car. Henry quickly flipped off the headlight.

He heard Isabel's muffled whimpers in the backseat. His mind raced. He sniffed the air. It was cold and smelled dank and musty. A shiver ran up his spine.

"What now?" Jeremy whispered into Henry's ear.

Henry spun around to check the hole in the wall. His eyes had adjusted to the dark, and he saw Titus's sharp claw still batting at the opening.

"We don't stand a hair of a chance against Titus," said Henry. "I'd rather try our luck here." He flicked the headlight back on and revved the engine. The rats backed away, but not by much. One of them snarled, showing his horribly yellowed teeth. Then they all moved toward the car.

Henry made the engine roar again.

"It's going to take more than that to chase us away," sneered the shifty-eyed rat with the yellow teeth. "This is our territory, and you don't belong!"

"Hang on!" Henry yelled as he pounded the pedal to the floor and drove straight at the rats. All five of them jumped clear of the car as Henry sped past them into the pitch-black tunnels and passageways beyond.

"Are they following?" Henry yelled over at Jeremy.

"Yes, but they're falling behind. Don't slow down!"

"Drive, Henry! Drive!" Isabel screamed.

"Where are we?" yelled Henry.

"How am I supposed to know?" Jeremy shouted.

"I don't like the looks of this tunnel," Henry shouted back.

Slow trickles of water oozed down the tunnel's slimy green walls, and the air was thick with the stench of garbage.

Henry jammed on the brakes when he caught sight of what lay ahead of them. There were swarms of rats as far as a snout could sniff.

At first, nobody moved.

"Those guys don't look too happy to see us," squeaked Jeremy, pointing to a group of particularly scruffy-looking rats emerging from the shadows and approaching them.

"Cat got your tongue?" snarled a rat with greasy fur and orange crumb-encrusted whiskers as he chucked an empty bag to the ground.

Henry scanned the crowd. All the other rats seemed to be keeping their distance from the pack that was slinking toward the car. "There must be nine—no, ten, eleven—of them!" he said, counting quickly. He wanted to tell Jeremy and Isabel what to do—or what not to do—but he didn't have a clue.

As the band of rats got closer, Henry realized how big they were. One of them lit a match and held it out toward the car. He turned and half smiled at the others, revealing a gap between his rotten teeth.

Some of the rats had scars; some were missing

the corner of an ear or the end of a tail. There was an especially scary-looking rat with a patch over one eye.

"Mighty nice set of wheels for your collection, wouldn't ya say, Snag?" said a rat missing part of his ear. The rat bent over and looked at himself in the side-view mirror and ran a paw through his grimy fur.

"I quite agree," Snag answered with a sneer as he ran his wrinkled paw down the length of the car. "Mighty fine!" Then he turned to look at Henry.

"You wouldn't mind if I take her for a little spin, would you now?"

Henry didn't think it was a question. He resisted the urge to twirl his twitching tail and tried to look Snag straight in the eye. "Of course not." He hated himself for trembling. He pushed open the door, and Snag moved aside, then he climbed out of the car, waving a paw to Jeremy and Isabel to follow.

Snag didn't hesitate. He squeezed himself into the driver's seat. The moment he was in, the rest of the pack fought fiercely for space.

Henry cringed as he watched them clamber all over the car, scratching its beautiful shiny paint with their claws and ripping through the soft leather seats. He noticed Snag staring blankly at all the dials and buttons on the dashboard until he finally found the starter button. Then something amazing happened. Snag hit the button over and over again, but the car wouldn't start. It was out of gas!

Snag got out, slammed the door, and whipped his powerful tail down on top of the car's hood. "What kind of trick is this?" he fumed. "You're messing with the wrong rat!"

As Henry stared wide-eyed up at Snag, he took a few steps backward. *This is it,* he thought. Henry's mind raced as he wondered what to do, but before he could come up with a solution, he heard a voice boom from behind him.

"Go stick your snout into someone else's business, Snag."

Henry spun around and saw a wizened rat who looked like he'd seen a lot more fighting in his day than Snag and the rest of his gang. Half his tail was missing, and he had jagged scars and gashes all over his body.

"You've got it wrong, Silver Snout," said Snag, making a deep growling sound as he narrowed his eyes threateningly. "I suggest you go back to where you came from before you get hurt."

Silver Snout walked right up to Snag and stopped, barely a whisker away.

"These mice may have crossed the territory line by coming here," said Silver Snout, "but they saved one of our own along the way."

Jeremy gave Henry a puzzled look, and for a

moment, Henry didn't understand either. Then it hit him. *The baby rat!* thought Henry. He let out a little puff of air.

"I don't like mice any more than you do," the elder rat continued, "but they saved my grandson from Titus, so I'm grateful."

Snag seemed to be ignoring the speech until Silver Snout grabbed him by the throat.

Nobody twitched a whisker.

ON THE COUNT OF THREE

"YOU GOT LUCKY THIS TIME," SNAG SNARLED after Silver Snout released him from his grip. He stared threateningly at Henry. "Don't think it will happen again. You better get going before your luck runs out."

Henry stood stock-still. He heard a few stifled squeaks from Isabel behind him. Jeremy stood by his side, planted like a statue.

Snag shot Henry one more look before he

skulked off, his rat pack following close behind.

Henry let out his breath.

"Can we go home now, Henry?" Isabel squeaked.

Jeremy and Henry exchanged a worried glance.

"We're going to have to leave the car here, Henry," Jeremy said, reading Henry's mind.

"We can't do that. I promised I'd bring it back."

"Promised who?" asked Jeremy.

"Myself, that's who! And besides, I don't want Warden to get suspicious if it's missing. He might search the drawers and discover my family living there."

"But how can we get it back where it belongs if it's out of gas?" Jeremy said. "We couldn't be farther from home if we tried." He tossed his paws hopelessly in the air.

For the first time since their adventure began, Henry felt exhausted. He pictured himself curled up on his soft bed of cotton balls and cattail fluff with the smell of poppy-seed pie wafting through the air. Then a bolt of fear suddenly gripped him, snapping him out of his daydream.

Henry felt a soft tap on his shoulder.

When he turned, Henry saw the baby rat standing behind him.

Silver Snout reached out and wrapped a paw around the young rat's shoulders. "This is my grandson. His name is Widget."

The young rat looked at Henry and smiled. "You saved me," he said. "That cat almost killed me, and you saved me."

"I'm afraid Widget got lost," Silver Snout explained. "He wandered off and got himself into a dangerous situation."

Widget's whiskers drooped and he looked down at his paws.

"That's what happened to me," squeaked Isabel

tenderly. "Henry and Jeremy saved me, too. Then we got chased down here by that horrible cat."

"Widget and I would like to return the favor and lend you a helping paw," said Silver Snout. "We can escort you back to the border of Rat Alley." Then the old rat turned and commanded: "All paws on deck!" And suddenly, dozens of rats from the crowd stepped out of the darkness.

"We owe these mice our help. Who is willing to push this car up to the border?"

A group of young, muscular-looking rats raised their tails to volunteer.

Henry clapped his paws together and patted Isabel on the back reassuringly. Maybe this nightmare was finally going to end.

Isabel and Widget jumped into the car. Isabel let Widget sit behind the steering wheel.

"Ready, boys?" hollered Silver Snout at the

back end of the car beside the other rats.

Even though Henry and Jeremy were so much smaller than the rats, they felt obliged to help—or at least look as if they were.

They joined the rats behind the car, and everyone leaned in to push.

⇥ 13 ⇤
SAFE PASSAGE

"THIS IS AS FAR AS WE CAN GO," SILVER Snout announced when they reached the border of Rat Alley.

Now they needed to hide the car from Snag and his pack, just in case. They buried it beneath a mound of moldy meat scraps, crinkled paper, crackly plastic bags, and smelly, slippery slime. Before they exchanged good-byes, Silver Snout asked, "Who among you is willing to stand guard until our friends can return for their car?"

Two rats, named Diesel and Dodger, volunteered.

"Well done, then!" said Silver Snout, turning to face Henry.

"Thank you," Henry said, looking up at Silver Snout and shaking his large paw. "Thank you for all your help. I don't know what would have happened if you hadn't come along."

At that moment, Henry had an idea. He thought it best to keep it quiet, so he pulled Silver Snout aside for a quick discussion while Isabel and Jeremy said their good-byes to Widget and the others. With a sigh of relief and a grateful smile, Henry turned to leave.

As the three of them made their way toward home, though, something kept nagging at the edges of Henry's mind. By the time they reached the familiar path back to the Whiskers' place, Henry realized what it was and stopped abruptly.

He turned and placed both paws on Isabel's petite shoulders.

"You have to go on by yourself, Izzy." He glanced at Jeremy and then continued. "If Jeremy and I go with you, Mother won't let us leave to get the car, and we *can't* leave the car. You go home so she knows we are all safe."

A frightened look flitted across Isabel's face. Her lower lip quivered. When tears escaped her control, Henry offered a calming thought. "If we're not back before the Mouse Masquerade, you can get Uncle Charlie to send out a search party. But don't say a word to anyone until then."

Isabel sniffled, nodded, and wiped her eyes. Henry gave her a brotherly embrace. He kissed her damp cheek and nudged her toward the crack in the floor above them.

As soon as Henry thought Isabel was safely home, he and Jeremy took a different route into the dollhouse so that Mother Mouse wouldn't see them.

"It's getting light out," Henry said, noticing the palest light peeking into the entrance of the exhibit room. "Hurry!"

Jeremy didn't answer. He didn't have to. Nighttime was slipping into day, and time was running out if they were going to return the car under the blanket of darkness. They headed straight for one of the bedrooms, hoping the hot water bottle was still in the place where Henry remembered seeing it.

"Here it is," exclaimed Henry. "Do you think this will hold enough gas to get us home?"

"It has to," squeaked Jeremy.

✦ 14 ✦
TITUS

DASHING BACK DOWN TO THE FLEET OF
cars, Henry and Jeremy scurried over to the gas
pump. "Fill 'er up!" Henry panted, holding the hot
water bottle out for Jeremy to place the nozzle in.
Hoping it would be enough to get them home,
they wasted no time getting back to the Rat Alley
border.

Sticking to the shadows as much as possible,
Henry took the lead. When the familiar mound

of muck appeared and they could see Diesel and Dodger pacing on the far side of the car, Henry held up a paw to signal Jeremy to stop. He cautiously sniffed for danger, then waved Jeremy on. They scampered over to the car, where the two rats met them to help dig it out from hiding. They filled the gas tank as quickly as possible and thanked Diesel and Dodger before rushing to leave.

"Ready to roll?" Henry whispered to Jeremy as he climbed into the driver's seat.

"You bet!" Jeremy replaced the gas cap and hopped in the car. He tossed the hot water bottle in the back, and Henry started the engine.

Just as the car began to inch forward, Isabel appeared out of nowhere, pumping her two front paws in the air. "Stop!" she hollered.

Henry braked and opened his mouth to say something, but nothing came out.

"Where did *you* come from?" squeaked Jeremy.

"I backtracked from home," Izzy replied, darting over to the side window next to Henry. "I'm so glad I got here in time," she panted. "When I got home, nobody was there, but Mother left this note," she gushed, handing Henry the note.

Henry read it out loud:

Not safe here.

Evacuate.

Gone to Uncle Charlie's.

Come immediately.

As soon as he'd finished reading it, Izzy continued. "The place is crawling with humans. I heard them. Lots of them. I got out of there as fast as possible, but I heard them say that today is the rain date for the queen's birthday banquet."

"What does that mean?" asked Henry.

"I don't know, but they said the party is TONIGHT!" Izzy puffed.

"That means . . ." Henry paused, trying to make

sense of it all. "That means that the masquerade has to be tonight!"

"We better get going," said Jeremy, clapping his paws.

"Just one second," squeaked Henry, hopping out of the car to chase after Diesel and Dodger. They hadn't gone far. He delivered his message and raced back to Isabel and Jeremy.

Izzy jumped into the backseat once again and held on for dear life as they sped off. Bumping along on the gravely ground through the tunnels, the three of them were too tired to talk. Then Jeremy asked, "How are we going to get the car back up that long staircase?"

Henry and Jeremy exchanged a worried glance and fell silent again.

"I know!" yelled Henry. "The elevator that I saw Warden get into right next to the stairs!" He held up a paw for Jeremy to high-five.

"Yes!" They slapped paws.

"We make a good team," said Henry, winking at Izzy's reflection in the rearview mirror.

The farther Henry drove, the more familiar the tunnels became. They all ran together, criss-crossing, intersecting, and snaking below Windsor Castle. He followed his instincts, and before long, they were spit out of a pipe behind a furnace in the basement corridor where they'd last seen Titus.

After poking their noses out to make sure it was safe, they cruised a short distance until they reached the elevator.

"I'll do it," Jeremy volunteered. He hopped out of the car, scaled up the wall, pressed the big shiny button, and dashed back down.

"How do we know they won't see us when we get upstairs?" asked Izzy.

"We have to take our chances," said Henry. "It's too early for visitors." He was thinking out loud.

"So the only humans we have to worry about are the ones working on the dollhouse," Jeremy piped in, reading Henry's mind.

"We'll take the car as far as we can and leave it where it will be found," said Henry. "That's the best we can do."

Jeremy nodded in agreement.

When the elevator doors opened, Henry eased the Silver Ghost inside. The doors closed, the elevator lurched, and then it lifted them up to the floor with the dollhouse exhibit. When the doors opened again, Titus was standing right in front of them.

Titus was so close to the elevator that Henry could smell his foul, sour breath. He glared at the three of them as if he had been waiting for them a long, long time. Titus flattened his ears and coiled himself into a crouch, ready to spring.

Henry revved the engine. Titus jumped up

on all fours. Henry punched the gas pedal and shot straight out of the elevator, right between Titus's legs.

"Bravo, Henry!" cheered Izzy, clinging to the seat.

Henry cranked the steering wheel and circled a huge statue on the far side of the room.

"Faster!" yelled Jeremy.

Henry stole a quick glimpse into his rear-view mirror just in time to see Titus's powerful paw slice through the air toward the car. With a neck-wrenching whack, the car was hurled into the air before it crashed to the floor and everything turned upside down.

✦ 15 ✦
MOUSE ON THE MEND

WHEN HENRY AWOKE, HE WAS WHISKER-to-whisker with a mouse who looked older than Windsor Castle itself. It was Dr. Getwell. Even though he looked blurry, Henry couldn't mistake his coat of thinning gray hair, oversized ears, and long, quivery whiskers bent every which way. Dr. Getwell was leaning over Henry, inspecting him from head to tail while his whiskers tickled Henry's nose.

"Well, look who's back to the land of the living," harrumphed the old mouse as he cleared his throat and straightened up. "Remember me, Henry?"

Henry began to nod his head but stopped abruptly. It hurt too much.

"Head hurt?" asked Dr. Getwell, digging into his medical bag.

Henry didn't say anything. He didn't remember climbing into bed and he couldn't imagine why Dr. Getwell was there, but he felt weak and tired so he stopped trying to think and closed his eyes. He heard Dr. Getwell speaking with someone, but the voices were whispered and muffled as Henry drifted back to sleep.

When Henry opened his eyes again, he was alone. It took a moment before he realized that he was in Jeremy's bedroom. *Why?* he wondered. The light was dim, but he could see from a nearby stool that somebody had been sitting by his bedside.

The nest was silent and still. *Must be late,* Henry thought as he tried to sit up. His body refused. The slightest movement made his stiff muscles scream and his head throb. He rubbed his brow gently.

A moment later, he heard someone scurrying outside the room.

"You're awake," whispered Mother Mouse, rushing to his side. "How are you feeling? Are you in much pain? Do you know where you are? Talk to me, Henry."

Henry was struggling to make sense of what his mother was saying. "What happened?" he moaned.

Mother Mouse sniffled. "Oh, Henry, I've been worried whiskerless about you," she said, starting to sob. "Don't you remember the accident?"

"Accident?" Henry frowned. "All I remember is seeing Titus take a swipe at us in the car and everything spinning around." An awful wave of panic washed over him. "Where is Izzy? Where's Jeremy? Are they all right?"

Mother Mouse scootched next to Henry on the bed and squeezed his paw. She smiled down at him. "They are both just fine. Jeremy has a sprained paw, but that's all, and your sister's out in the kitchen telling everyone what happened." She hesitated to go on.

"What is it? What's wrong?" Henry asked, watching her face for clues.

Mother Mouse stood and squeaked softly, "You're going to be fine, but you broke your leg." She pulled back the covers for Henry to see. He lifted his head off the pillow to inspect his leg. Dr. Getwell had custom nibbled two lollypop sticks to brace either side of it. A string of bright red yarn was wrapped around the sticks to form a cast.

Mother Mouse covered his leg again and began to cry. "Oh, Henry, I was so afraid. I don't know what I would do if anything happened to you. Thank you for bringing Isabel back and coming home safely to me." She leaned over and kissed him softly on his forehead. She plumped his pillow for him as he leaned back against it.

"Dr. Getwell said that you should be able to walk with your cast, and you'll probably be able to dance a little if you're careful." Mother Mouse sounded cheerier.

"At the masquerade?" asked Henry. He had completely forgotten about it.

"Yes, Henry, tonight!" Mother Mouse clapped her paws and smiled. "Those people have been working nonstop to get everything repaired and polished so they could put things back in place before they leave to help with the queen's party. I just took a peek. Everyone's gone. It sparkles like new, and the party can go on just as your father would have wanted." She stroked his cheek with the back of her paw.

Just then, Isabel darted into the room. She looked so happy and carefree.

"They're coming," she squeaked excitedly. "Can I hide in your bed?" But before Henry could answer, Isabel burrowed her way into the loose feathers and fluff and asked Henry not to give her away.

A smile crept across his face, and Mother Mouse smiled back. When all of Henry's sisters and brothers tried to run in, she held up her paw, saying Henry needed his rest. When they had all skittered away, Henry poked Izzy. She popped her head out and sniffed the air.

"All gone," he whispered with a faint smile.

Isabel hugged Henry. "You're my hero," she whispered in his ear, then she kissed him on the cheek, jumped out of the bed, and dashed out of sight.

Henry dozed on and off the rest of the day. By the time Jeremy poked his head in to check on him, he was feeling a lot better. He rather liked the looks of his cast and even looked forward to showing it off a little bit at the Mouse Masquerade.

"How are you?" Henry asked when he saw Jeremy's bandaged paw.

"Better than you." Jeremy smiled. "You sure had everyone worried. Let's not do that again!"

"What happened, anyway?" asked Henry. "I can't remember a thing after Titus whacked the car."

"It's a pretty good story, my friend," said Jeremy, sitting down on the stool. He gushed the whole thing from beginning to end while Henry listened, transfixed. At first, it felt like he was listening to an adventure that had nothing to do with him, but as Jeremy went on, memories returned.

"But how did we escape?" asked Henry. "And what happened to the car?"

"We were thrown from the car." Jeremy looked at Henry, and Henry looked back wide-eyed. "You were knocked out. Izzy and I pulled you through a floor grate before Titus could get to us, and I ran to get help. You were still unconscious when Uncle Charlie and I came back for you. The two of us carried you here."

Henry couldn't believe it. He sat in stunned silence, listening to how his friend had saved his life. And little Izzy, too!

Jeremy went on. "You haven't heard the best part. Warden and Freddy found Titus playing with the car after we escaped, so he got blamed for taking it and scratching it all up. I overheard them say that it would be freshly painted and returned to the dollhouse."

Jeremy beamed at Henry. "We couldn't have planned it better if we'd tried!" he said, slapping his tail on the floor and laughing out loud.

Henry was speechless. He couldn't believe their luck. A sense of drowsy relief washed over him. Then he remembered the one thing that nobody else could.

↠ 16 ↞
FINISHING TOUCHES

"I INVITED SILVER SNOUT AND WIDGET TO the Mouse Masquerade," Henry told Jeremy as they made their way up to the Whiskers'.

"You what?" Jeremy half choked out. He looked at Henry and shook his head. "This is going to be an interesting night," he chuckled.

When they reached the kitchen, everyone was clustered around the table. Henry's sisters and brothers were putting the final touches on their masks. The nibbling and gnawing stopped when they saw Henry hobble into the room. Isabel scampered over to him.

"Can you tell who I am?" she asked as she slipped her mask on.

"Not a chance," Henry assured her, suddenly remembering how he'd asked Father the same question once. A wave of sadness overwhelmed him.

"I didn't think so," exclaimed Isabel, scrambling back to her workstation at the table.

Henry quickly wiped his eyes.

"I hope you don't mind, Henry, but I went ahead and made you a mask while you were recovering in bed." Mother Mouse smiled knowingly at Henry, then added, "Just in case."

How did she know he would decide to go? Henry wondered as he extended a paw to get a better look.

"I made it match the color of your cast. Royal

red! I nibbled it from the bishop's church robe myself." Mother Mouse beamed.

Henry peered down at the velvety mask he held in his paws. Surrounding the eyeholes were shiny gold sequins, and purple satin ribbons were attached as tie strings. It was the best-looking mask he had ever seen. Henry looked up and noticed that his brothers and sisters had stopped their work to watch.

"Put it on! Put it on!" they all pleaded and cheered. So he slowly lifted the mask to his face.

"Here, I'll help," offered Regina, grabbing the satiny ties in her paws and securing the mask on Henry's head.

Paws clapped enthusiastic approval all around. When Henry removed the mask, he limped over to kiss Mother Mouse and thank her.

Mother gave Henry a quick hug and leaned in close to whisper, "Your father would be so proud of you, Henry." She squeezed him tightly. Just then, music from the queen's party could be heard floating through the castle floorboards of the royal banquet hall above. Mother Mouse released Henry and clapped her paws together.

"Hurry up, children. That's the signal. The coast is clear. We'd better be going. Our guests will be arriving soon."

✦ 17 ✦

MOUSE MASQUERADE

HENRY SLIPPED HIS MASK ON AND FELL IN line between Mother Mouse and Regina, who was wearing a shockingly pink mask with a large feather sticking up and out of it. Following the tradition started by his father, the Whiskers family formed a receiving line to meet and greet each member of the mouse community as they entered the dollhouse. As the oldest child, Henry stood near the front.

Normally, he would enjoy the honor, but Henry was beginning to doubt whether he should have invited his surprise guests.

What if Mother Mouse throws them out? Or there's trouble? Henry worried. But before he could give it any more thought, mice streamed into the dollhouse and began shaking his paw, one after another.

"What happened to you, lad?" asked several mice.

"Did you get caught in a trap?" asked others.

"Oh, you poor dear," squeaked several motherly mice.

Henry had nearly reached his limit when Mother Mouse tapped him on the back with her tail.

"Would you like to excuse yourself and go see your friends?" she asked.

Henry let out a heavy sigh of relief and limped out of line and over to a nearby pillar. He leaned against it for support and watched while the band, called the Jester's Jig, warmed up their instruments. Light twinkled from the lanterns suspended from the ceiling and glistened off the newly polished statues of knights in shining armor. The floor, made of lapis blue and white marble, was open and spacious and provided ample room for mice to mingle and dance.

"Keeping an eye out?" asked Jeremy, coming over from the receiving line.

Henry nodded. "You don't suppose everyone's going to get their whiskers in a knot when they see our special guests, do you?" He noticed that his own voice was sounding worried.

"*Our* guests?" asked Jeremy. "*I* didn't invite them!"

"It'll be all right," Henry attempted reassuringly.

Jeremy shrugged his shoulders and gave Henry a faint smile, suggesting to Henry that he wasn't convinced.

"Right!" Henry rubbed his front paws together as if he were coming up with a better plan. "I guess we'll find out soon enough, then, won't we?" His stomach flip-flopped a little as he cast a glance at the growing crowd.

The two of them stood near the pillar taking in the scene. While the queen's guests could be heard gathering upstairs in the royal halls of Windsor Castle, masked mice of all ages scampered onto the dance floor of the dollhouse below. The band began to play, and everyone picked up their paws to dance. Music from both parties mingled in the air, creating an especially festive atmosphere.

Henry tried to relax as he watched silver-haired mice twirl and glide across the smooth marble floor in each other's paws. Younger mice seemed to hear a different beat as they jiggled and jumped to the music. Most every mouse wore a mask or unusual headdress. Some were made from paper and string, while others were fashioned from snippets nibbled from royal robes.

Every year, Henry and Jeremy played a game in which they awarded imaginary prizes for the most original, bizarre, unique, and outrageous creations of the evening.

The party was in full swing when the music suddenly stopped and they heard a collective gasp.

"From the sound of it, I'd say your guests have arrived," Jeremy whispered into Henry's ear.

Guests seemed to be retreating. Several darted out of sight. Henry snapped into focus. When he turned toward the entrance, he saw Silver Snout and Widget standing tall and towering above the mice.

"You better do something, Henry, before this gets out of control," Jeremy said.

Henry scanned the room in search of Mother Mouse, but he couldn't see her through the flurry of confused mice running to and fro. He realized that Jeremy was right. He had to calm the crowd.

Henry hobbled toward the marble staircase, and when he reached the bottom step, he turned to face everyone.

"Ahem." He cleared his throat. "May I have your attention?"

Only a few mice near him seemed to notice that he was attempting to make a speech. Twirling his tail around one paw, Henry climbed to a higher step and spoke up again, a little louder this time.

"Excuse me," he nearly shouted. "May I have your attention, please?"

Just getting the first few words out made it easier to breathe, and his shoulders began to relax.

Mice on the floor below him began elbowing one another and twitching their ears, waiting to hear what he was about to say. Of course, he had no idea himself. He hadn't exactly planned to say *anything*, but words began to flow anyway.

"I'd like to start by thanking all of you for coming this evening," Henry began. Everyone turned to listen, and the room fell silent. "It would have made my father very happy to know that you are continuing this tradition of gathering together in this special house that we Whiskers get to call home."

Henry noticed smiles growing across several snouts and was encouraged. He took a deep breath and continued, just as he noticed Mother Mouse clasping her paws in front of her and looking at him with wide eyes.

"As many of you know, my father lost his life saving the lives of others." Henry paused and swallowed the lump in his throat. All eyes were on him. "Which is why," Henry continued, "my father would want you to join me in welcoming two very special guests here this evening." Henry motioned to Jeremy to bring Silver Snout and Widget over to him.

All at once, the crowd turned to look at the oversized rodents in their midst. They separated to make way as Jeremy led the two strangers toward the grand staircase. As the group approached, Henry saw Isabel and Mother Mouse slip through the crowd to meet up with Jeremy, Silver Snout, and Widget at the bottom of the steps.

"If it weren't for Silver Snout and Widget"— Henry gestured toward the two smiling rats—"I wouldn't be here tonight." Henry paused again. "They saved my life . . . all our lives." He pointed to Jeremy and Isabel, who moved over to stand next to Widget.

Mother Mouse looked stunned and confused. There was a flurry of gasps and excited squeaks. Henry raised a paw to silence everyone before he continued.

"So please join me in welcoming and thanking our newest friends and honored guests, Silver Snout and his grandson Widget."

At first, there was silence, then Mother Mouse turned, smiled at Henry, and began to clap. One by one, everyone joined in until a thunder of applause filled the room. Mice, young and old, pounded their paws together and cheered wildly. Mother Mouse beamed proudly up at Henry and then gave Silver Snout a grateful hug. Strangers were patting Jeremy on the back, hugging Isabel, and pushing past one another to come shake paws with the rats.

When the band finally struck up their instruments again, Isabel was the first to step out onto the dance floor, pulling Widget along with her. Mother Mouse and Silver Snout followed, then everybody eagerly hopped onto the dance floor. The house practically quaked in lively celebration.

Henry watched, amazed and relieved, as everyone jittered to the beat. Then Regina appeared at his side. "May I have this dance?" she asked. Henry nodded an enthusiastic yes and let her help him down the stairs. Mice made way for them as they walked to the center of the room, and everyone patted Henry on the back as he passed by. For the first time in days, Henry felt a burst of excitement and energy as he lifted his tail high and joined in the dance.

✦ ACKNOWLEDGMENTS ✦

THANK YOU TO EVERY PERSON—FAMILY, friend, or acquaintance—that has ever encouraged me in any way. You have helped me *Believe* (with a capital *B*). What a gift! I hope to pay it forward every day.

More specifically I want to thank my editor, Alyson Heller, for finding joy in Henry Whiskers and choosing to adopt him into the Aladdin/ Simon & Schuster family. Your cheerful input has made his story better and is greatly appreciated. And thank you to my agent, Ginger Knowlton, for adopting *me* and guiding me through this new journey. Thanks, too, to my UK writing group, Mary, Deb, Lisa, Sue, Joy, Ellie, and Linda, as well as my writing mentor, Patricia Reilly Giff; freelance

~ *Acknowledgments* ~

editor, Rachel Klein; and my first test case, James Kontulis, along with Erica Bergmans and Melissa Thorkilsen for all your help. Nothing is accomplished by one's self.

Here's a sneak peek at HENRY'S next adventure!

A MAP

HENRY WHISKERS SUCKED IN HIS BREATH and clamped a paw over his mouth. His rounded ears flicked back and forth—listening for any sign of trouble. Certain it was safe to continue, he raised the crumpled wad of paper to his nose and sniffed its musty nooks and crannies, then gently uncrinkled it and spread it out on the desk. His whiskers twitched with anticipation as he smoothed away its wrinkles. His heart ticked faster. This was BIG! He could *feel* it! Right down to the tip of his tail.

A milky white moon hung in the sky above Windsor Castle. Visitors and tour guides had long since gone home, including Warden, the tour guide in the exhibit room of the world's most famous dollhouse. Sitting on its base, raised to eye level for visitors to view, Queen Mary's Dollhouse glowed like a jewel in the middle of the dimly lit room. Standing five feet tall, eight feet long, and four feet wide, it made the perfect place for a family of mice to call home.

The dollhouse was never meant for dolls or even for children to play with. It worked like a real home fit for a queen, complete with four floors, forty rooms, two working elevators, hot and cold running water, and electricity. Everything was made to be dollhouse-size, including a grand marble staircase, a kitchen with shiny copper pots, a garage filled with luxury cars, and toilets that really flushed. Even crystal chandeliers that twinkled, a grandfather clock that chimed, and a library filled with leather-bound books were crafted like the life-size copies found in England's finest homes, so it was no wonder that nearly a million people came to see the dollhouse every year. But the one thing they'd never seen were the mice that nested among the empty cedar storage drawers built into the base. Twenty-four generations of Whiskers had lived there, tucked safely out of sight. Henry was the twenty-fifth in a long line of Henry Whiskers.

The night belonged to Henry! It was the ONLY time Mother Mouse allowed him to roam the dollhouse, and now he was convinced that he was onto *something*!

Only moments ago, he had been reading, sprawled across his favorite leather armchair in the library, when something caught his eye. It was the shiny brass handles on the desk drawers nearby. He had an idea. He lassoed the book with his tail, hopped out of the chair, and stuffed the book back into place on the bookshelf. On the desk there was a collection of fountain pens, leather-bound boxes, silver boxes, smoking pipes, and stationery. *Nothing can look out of place,* he reminded himself while his paws itched to touch each of them.

Henry swung his tail out from under his body and sat in the desk chair. He ran a forepaw across the smooth walnut surface of the desk and noticed that the pens, letter openers, and a crystal bottle filled with blue ink were embossed with the queen's crown, just like the life-size versions that Her Royal Highness used. Photographs of people stood framed in sterling silver, smiling back at him. *Feels like they are watching me,* he thought, as he clasped a shiny drawer handle and gave it a little tug. The drawer glided halfway out and got stuck. Upon inspection, Henry spied a piece of crumpled paper jammed in the back. Careful not to rip it, he eased it out. He saw several scratchy paw-drawn images connected by lines and dots on the paper flattened in front of him. Instantly he recognized the Copper Horse and the paved path leading up to it, called the Long Walk. He'd seen them a hundred times from the castle's front windows. There were other things he didn't recognize, but they had words like *Totem Pole* and *Gardens* written next to them. To the left of all of them, near the ragged edge, Henry noticed a large mysterious *X.*

Henry's heart thumped faster as he studied the map more closely. His heart nearly stopped when he spotted some small initials scratched on the lower right corner.

He slapped a paw over his mouth again. He could hardly contain himself. A flood of questions swirled through his mind. *How could he have . . . ? When did he . . . ? I wonder if . . . ? Does Mother . . . ?* Then it struck him. He had to show Jeremy NOW!

Henry swiftly rolled up the map and wound his tail around it. He slammed the desk drawer shut, leaped out of the chair, and shoved it back into place. He gave the desk and the room one final inspection, then dashed off to find his best friend.

He's probably in the castle kitchens, Henry guessed, picturing Jeremy—who was also his distant cousin—nibbling away on crumbs from the queen's dinner much earlier that night. Henry hopped out of the dollhouse and onto the exhibit room floor. Navigating his way through the castle, he took all the shortcuts he knew, racing through the heating ducts until he reached Lantern Lobby, just outside the biggest kitchen of them all. He poked his head out of a grate in the wall to check for Titus, the steely-eyed tabby cat who roamed around as if he owned the place. When Henry was certain that the coast was clear, he hopped out of the grate and darted across the floor toward the kitchen.

Twenty mouse lengths away from the kitchen door that he planned to slip under, Henry heard a *clack-clack-clack*ing. It was the unmistakable sound of cat claws on the hard stone floor. Henry crouched, frozen to the spot, not daring to look or twitch a whisker. When he heard the clacking gather speed, he knew Titus had spotted him. Henry held his breath and made a run for it, slipping under the kitchen door just in time, leaving the nasty old fur ball hissing on the other side.

Henry sprang up onto all four paws as fast as he could and sprinted for cover under one of the massive black iron ovens. He huffed and puffed until he caught his breath, then surveyed the enormous kitchen in search of Jeremy.

The floor was bathed in moonlight that poured through the windows high above. Its gleam bounced off the copper pots and kettles that lined the wall shelves and ringed the giant room. The very edges of the kitchen offered safe cover in the shadows cast by ovens, stoves, and worktables.

"Henry!" hollered Jeremy. "Over here!"

Henry turned toward the sound and eagerly waved the map for Jeremy to see, but Jeremy had turned away. Sitting in the middle of the open floor, spotlighted by moonshine, Jeremy looked like he didn't have a care in the world as he nibbled away on some whisker-wetting prize clutched in his over-size paws.

"Jeremy!" Henry yelled again. "Look what I found!" He scampered out from cover and stopped to reconsider.

"Come on!" Jeremy was signaling for Henry to come join him, but Henry shook his head no. He was anxious to show Jeremy the map, but something told him to stay in the shadows.

Henry curled his tail around the map and made his way closer to Jeremy by hugging the wall behind the ovens and stoves. When he was midway along, he cocked his ears and fixed his eyes on Jeremy. Something didn't feel right. "Jeremy!" he shouted, but it was no use. Jeremy zigged and zagged back and forth across the floor, following his nose in search of more crumbs. Henry shook his head, then all of a sudden, with no warning at all, the entire kitchen was flooded with bright fluorescent light.

Two cooks wearing white aprons, black-and-white-checkered pants, and black rubber-soled clogs marched in carrying black cases that reminded Henry of suitcases from the dollhouse, just a whole lot bigger. Henry's heart leaped into his throat. He looked back and forth between the cooks and Jeremy, who had tucked himself into a tight ball below a table, just a few tail lengths away from one of the cook's feet. In the middle of the kitchen, there was nowhere to run without being seen. No wall to hug. No vent to hop into. No drain to duck down. No stove or refrigerator to hide under. Henry could hardly breathe. *Look at me, look at me,* he willed Jeremy, but at that very moment, the black clog shifted and kicked Jeremy.

Jeremy shot out from under the table. The lady cook screeched and dropped her case, which crashed to the floor. An assortment of shiny, sharp kitchen knives—large and small—sprayed into the air and showered down all around Jeremy. He stopped still in his tracks.

Henry jumped out from under the stove. "Run Jeremy, run!"

Henry attempted to back up into the shadows again, but his legs felt heavy and wouldn't obey. The room began to swirl in front of his eyes as Jeremy stayed frozen to the same spot, surrounded by knives.

Thwap! Whop! Whap! The familiar sound of a broom came close to Henry's head, blowing his whiskers back. Jeremy sprang in and out of Henry's view as he scampered, hopped, and skittered away from the attacking broom.

"Stop, you'll kill 'im!" Henry heard the woman shriek.

"That's the idea, milady!" the man shouted.

"Don't kill 'em, poor things. Let's trap 'em, and I'll trot 'em off tuh the park to set 'em free."

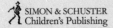

Did you LOVE reading this book?

Visit the Whyville...

IN THE MIDDLE BOOK HIVE

Where you can:

- Discover great books!
- Meet new friends!
- Read exclusive sneak peeks and more!

Log on to visit now!
bookhive.whyville.net